A Feiwel and Friends Book
An Imprint of Macmillan

HILL AND HOLE ARE BEST FRIENDS. Text copyright © 2016 by Kyle Mewburn. Illustrations copyright © 2016 by Vasanti Unka. All rights reserved. First published in the United States in 2016 by Feiwel and Friends. Originally published in New Zealand in 2010 by Puffin Books. Printed in China by Toppan Leefung Printing Ltd., Dongguan City, Guangdong Province. For information, address Feiwel and Friends, 175 Fifth Avenue, New York, N.Y. 10010.

Our books may be purchased in bulk for promotional, educational, or business use. Please contact your local bookseller or the Macmillan Corporate and Premium Sales Department at (800) 221-7945 ext. 5442 or by e-mail at MacmillanSpecialMarkets@macmillan.com

Library of Congress Cataloging-in-Publication Data
Names: Mewburn, Kyle, author. | Unka, Vasanti, illustrator.
Title: Hill & Hole are best friends / Kyle Mewburn ; illustrated by Vasanti Unka.
Description: First edition. | New York : Feiwel and Friends, 2016. | Summary: "Hill and Hole were best friends. Hill likes being a hill, and Hole likes being a hole, but sometimes they wonder what it would be like to swap places. Maybe Mole and Wind can help?"— Provided by publisher. | Summary: Two friends, a hill and a hole, long to be more like one another.
Identifiers: LCCN 2015031040 | ISBN 9781250076373 (hardcover)
Subjects: | CYAC: Best friends—Fiction. | Friendship—Fiction. | Mountains—Fiction. | Holes—Fiction.
Classification: LCC PZ7.M56794 Hi 2016 | DDC [E]—dc23
LC record available at http://lccn.loc.gov/2015031040.

Feiwel and Friends logo designed by Filomena Tuosto

First Edition—2016

The artist used a combination of watercolor and digital techniques to create the illustrations in this book.

10 9 8 7 6 5 4 3 2 1

mackids.com

Hill & Hole
Are Best Friends

Kyle Mewburn

illustrated by **Vasanti Unka**

FEIWEL AND FRIENDS | NEW YORK

Hill and Hole

are best friends.

Every morning, Hole asked Hill,

"What can you see, so far away?"

"I can see the sun rising," Hill replied. "It looks like another **beautiful** day."

Every evening, Hill asked Hole,

"What can you feel, so deep in the ground?"

"I can feel the earth breathing," Hole replied.

"It feels like another **peaceful** night."

Hole liked being a hole.
But sometimes,
he imagined himself as a hill.

How amazing it must be
to see the **sun rising.**

Hill liked being a hill, too.
But sometimes,
he dreamed of being a hole.

How wonderful it must be
to feel the **earth breathing.**

So one day, Hill and Hole asked Mole,
"Can you make Hole a hill, and Hill a hole?"

"Indeed I can," said Mole.
"Isn't a hole just an inside-out hill,
and a hill but an upside-down hole?"

mole dug and dug...

"Thank you, Mole," said Hill the hole.

"Thank you, Mole," said Hole the hill.

That morning, Hill the hole asked Hole the hill,

"Can you see the sun rising?"

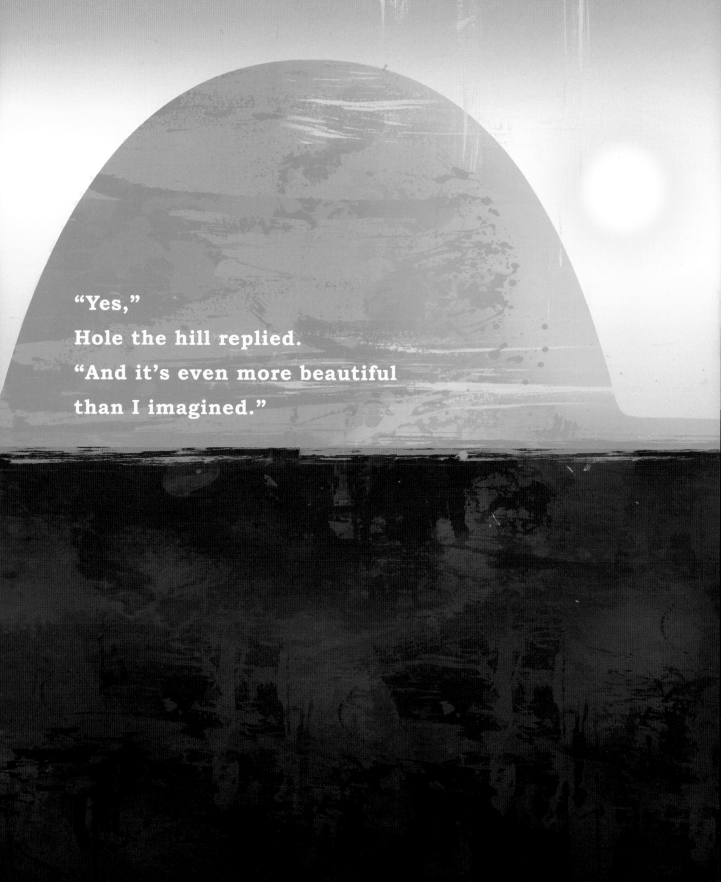

"Yes,"
Hole the hill replied.
"And it's even more beautiful
than I imagined."

"**Can you** feel the earth breathing?"

"Yes,"
Hill the hole replied.
"And it's even more peaceful
than I thought it would be."

And they were very happy . . .

for a while.

But one day,
Hill the hole asked Hole the hill,
"Can you see the sun rising?"

"Yes," Hole the hill said.
"It's very beautiful, but . . .
sometimes I can see so far
it **frightens** me.

"I miss being a hole."

Then Hole the hill asked Hill the hole,
"Do you feel the earth breathing?"

"Yes," Hill the hole said.
"It's very peaceful, but . . .
sometimes I feel it so strongly
it **scares** me.

"I miss being a hill."

So Hole the hill and Hill the hole asked Wind,
"Can you make us Hill and Hole again?"

"I'll try my best," said Wind.
"But sometimes it's easier to do things
than to *undo* them once they're done."

Wind blew

and blew...

. . . until there was no hole and there was no hill,
just a vast, flat plain stretching all the way to the horizon.

"That's the best I can do," said Wind.

Hole was neither hole *nor* hill.
And Hill wasn't hill *or* hole. But they didn't mind.

Every morning, they watched the sun rising together.
Every evening, they both felt the earth breathing.

And they were very happy . . .

for a while.